Dear Parent:

Congratulations! Your child is taking the first steps on an exciting journey. The destination? Independent reading!

STEP INTO READING® will help your child get there. The program offers five steps to reading success. Each step includes fun stories and colorful art. There are also Step into Reading Sticker Books, Step into Reading Math Readers, Step into Reading Write-In Readers, Step into Reading Phonics Readers, and Step into Reading Phonics First Steps! Boxed Sets—a complete literacy program with something for every child.

Learning to Read, Step by Step!

Ready to Read   Preschool–Kindergarten
• big type and easy words • rhyme and rhythm • picture clues
For children who know the alphabet and are eager to begin reading.

Reading with Help   Preschool–Grade 1
• basic vocabulary • short sentences • simple stories
For children who recognize familiar words and sound out new words with help.

Reading on Your Own   Grades 1–3
• engaging characters • easy-to-follow plots • popular topics
For children who are ready to read on their own.

Reading Paragraphs   Grades 2–3
• challenging vocabulary • short paragraphs • exciting stories
For newly independent readers who read simple sentences with confidence.

Ready for Chapters   Grades 2–4
• chapters • longer paragraphs • full-color art
For children who want to take the plunge into chapter books but still like colorful pictures.

STEP INTO READING® is designed to give every child a successful reading experience. The grade levels are only guides. Children can progress through the steps at their own speed, developing confidence in their reading, no matter what their grade.

Remember, a lifetime love of reading starts with a single step!

Tales from
the Tracks

Thomas the Tank Engine & Friends™

CREATED BY BRITT ALLCROFT

Based on The Railway Series by The Reverend W Awdry.
© 2009 Gullane (Thomas) LLC.
Thomas the Tank Engine & Friends and Thomas & Friends are trademarks of
Gullane (Thomas) Limited.
HIT and the HIT Entertainment logo are trademarks of HIT Entertainment Limited.

HIT entertainment

www.randomhouse.com/kids
www.thomasandfriends.com

ISBN: 978-0-375-85545-0

Printed in the United States of America
10 9 8 7 6 5 4 3 2 1

THOMAS & FRIENDS™

Tales from the Tracks

Based on *The Railway Series*
by the Reverend W Awdry

Illustrated by Richard Courtney

Step 1 and Step 2 Books
A Collection of Six Early Readers

Random House 🏠 New York

Contents

Thomas
Goes Fishing

Thomas chugged
by the river.
He saw children fishing.

"Peep, peep,"
Thomas said.

The children waved.

13

"I wish to fish,"
said Thomas.

"An engine fishing,"
the Driver said.
"That is funny!"

Each day Thomas
saw the children.
Each day Thomas
wished to fish.

One day
Thomas stopped.

"Oh, dear!" he said.

"My boiler hurts!"

The Driver looked

in the boiler.

It was empty.

The Driver filled
Thomas' boiler
with water
from the river.

Soon they were
chugging along.

Thomas stopped again.
"Hee hee!" said Thomas.

"My boiler feels funny."

The Driver looked
in the boiler.
It was not empty.

There was water
in the boiler.
That was not all!
There were fish, too!

Thomas had an idea.

He peeped loudly.

The children came

to see Thomas.

The children could fish
in the river!

The Driver could fish in Thomas!

And that is what
they did.

36

"Peep! Peep!"

THOMAS & FRIENDS™

The Close Shave

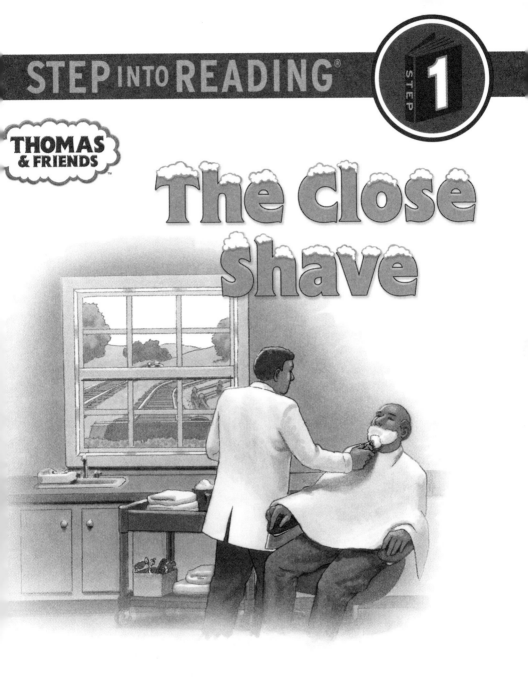

Thomas and Duck
are friends.

They are
not friends with the
Troublesome Trucks.

They like

to chug up hills.

They like
to zip down hills.

One day,
Duck was zipping
down a hill.
Hello, Thomas!

Duck heard
a warning whistle.

"Peeeeeep! Peeeeeep!"

Trucks had run away

from Thomas.

Go, Duck!

No! Trucks!

The Trucks
bumped Duck.

Mad Duck!

Glad Trucks!

Duck and the Trucks
rushed down the hill.

Duck saw

the end of the line.

Duck had to stop!

Duck crashed
into the barber shop.

Sad Duck!

Bad Trucks!

57

The barber

was cross.

Soapy Duck.

Dopey Trucks!

"I am sorry,"
said Duck.

"I had to stop
the runaway Trucks."

No one was hurt.

The shop could be fixed.

Duck was a hero!

Duck got cleaned up.

65

The Trucks
got picked up.

Duck had
a close shave!

Gordon's New View

Gordon was big.

Gordon was tall.

Gordon liked his view

from the Yard.

Gordon liked his view
from the stations, too.

He could see people.

People could see him.

"Gordon, you must go
to the new station,"
said Sir Topham Hatt.

Gordon rushed

to the new station.

He stopped inside.

There was no view.
Gordon could not see
the people.
They could not see him.

The next day,
Gordon was busy.
He pulled
the Express.

He rushed
to the Docks.

He raced back
to the new station.

He was in a hurry.

But his brakes were stuck.

He could not slow down.

Crash!

Gordon crashed
into the bumper.

Smash!

Gordon smashed
into the wall.

Now people could see him.
But Gordon could not
see them.
His eyes were shut tight.

The breakdown train
pulled Gordon back.

"Gordon, go to the Works,"
said Sir Topham Hatt.

When Gordon came back,
he was fixed.

93

The wall was fixed, too.
It had
a new window.

Gordon likes
his new view.

He can see people . . .

. . . and people can see him.

"Peep, peep!"

THOMAS
and PERCY
and the
DRAGON

It is night.

Percy is sleepy.

He is thinking about

the parade tomorrow.

Percy hears a rumble.

Something is coming.

Percy opens his eyes.

He sees a dragon.

It is big and yellow

and <u>scary</u>!

"Oh no!" cries Percy.

He shuts his eyes tight.

The rumble fades.

Percy peeks.

The dragon is

running away!

The next day,
Percy rushes
into the station.

"I saw a dragon
last night!" he says.

"Scared little Percy!"
teases James.
"You are off your tracks!"

James chugs off.

"Peep, peep, peep!"

"You just had

a bad dream . . .

. . . dragons are not real,"
says Edward.

Percy sees Thomas.
There is something
behind him.

It is big and yellow

and <u>scary</u>!

"Watch out, Thomas!"
shouts Percy.

"There is a dragon

chasing you!"

"Silly Percy,"
laughs Thomas.
"This dragon
will not eat you.

It is a paper dragon
for the parade."

Later, Thomas and Percy
stop to watch the parade.

There is Sir Topham Hatt.

Next comes a band.

"Here comes the dragon,"
says Thomas.

"He is <u>not</u> so scary

anymore,"

says Percy.

"You were brave to tell
me about it,"
says Thomas.

"It is good
   to tell someone,"
says Percy.

Henry
and the Elephant

Thomas left the Yard.

He went to run

his own Branch Line.

Henry and Gordon
missed Thomas.

With Thomas gone,
there was more
work to do.
Henry and Gordon
were cross.

Henry grumbled
as he pushed trucks.
Gordon grumbled
as he pulled coaches.

One day,
a circus came
to town.

Now the engines were even busier.

Henry pushed
the trucks.
Gordon pulled
the coaches.

They did not
grumble.
Henry and Gordon
liked the circus.

The next day,
Henry took workmen
to a blocked tunnel.

The workmen
picked up their tools.
"Time to clear the line."

They walked inside.

Something big was
in the tunnel.
It would not move.
It grunted.
It was alive!

They ran outside.

The Foreman had a plan.
Henry could push trucks
into the tunnel.

"Wheesh," said Henry.

Henry did not like

tunnels.

He was scared.

Henry pushed the
trucks.
They went
into the dark tunnel.
BUMP!

Henry pushed hard.
The big, scary thing
pushed back.

Henry pushed harder.
The big, scary thing
pushed hardest!
Henry inched
backwards.

First,

Henry was pushed

out of the tunnel.

Then the trucks

were pushed out.

At last,

they saw what

was in the tunnel.

It was an elephant!
And he looked cross.
He had run away
from the circus.

The workmen fed him
and gave him
lots of water.
The elephant felt better.

Henry felt better, too.

He let off steam.

Whoosh!

Henry's steam scared
the elephant.
Splash!
Poor Henry.

It was time to go home.
Everyone laughed
at Henry.

"An elephant
pushed me and
splashed me,"
Henry grumbled.

But in the Shed,
Henry told
his funny story.
His friends laughed.
This time
Henry laughed, too.

James Goes Buzz, Buzz

It was a sunny day.

Chirp! Chirp!

sang the birds.

Buzz! Buzz!

hummed the bees.

Trevor the Tractor Engine
was hard at work.

Chug! Chug!

James pulled up.

"Hello, Trevor,"

said James.

"You look as busy

as a bee."

"I am!" said Trevor.

Buzz! Buzz!

"What is that noise?"

asked James.

"Bees," said Trevor.

"I am taking this beehive

to the station."

Buzz! Buzz!

buzzed the bees.

"Bees are very loud!"
said James.
"Do not make them mad,"
said Trevor.
"They may sting you!"

"Hmmmph!" said James.
"I am not scared of
a bunch of bees!"
James puffed off.

The next day,
James chugged into
the station.
He saw boxes
and bundles
and bags.
And there was
the beehive!

People rushed
this way and that.
BUMP!
A porter bumped
into the beehive!

The beehive broke!

Buzz! Buzz!

The bees buzzed

around the station.

Buzz! Buzz!
The bees buzzed
around James.
"Buzz buzz off!"
said James.
The bees
did not listen.

The bees buzzed onto
James' hot boiler.
One of the bees
burned his foot.
Buzz! Buzz! Buzz!
The bee was angry.

He stung James

on the nose!

"Eeeeeeeeek,"
tooted James.
"Bad bee!"
James tried to make
the bees buzz off.

Chug! Chug!
James chugged
out of the station.

Whoosh!

He spun around

on the turntable.

Buzz! Buzz!

The bees liked the breeze.

Splash!

He tried to wash

them off.

Buzz! Buzz!

The bees took a bath.

Puff! Puff!
James blew smoke
at the bees.
Buzz! Buzz!
The bees did not budge.

James had an idea.

He turned around.

He chugged back
to find Trevor.

Buzz! Buzz!

The bees were home.

They buzzed back

into a beehive.

"Good bees!" said James.

"Goodbye, bees!"

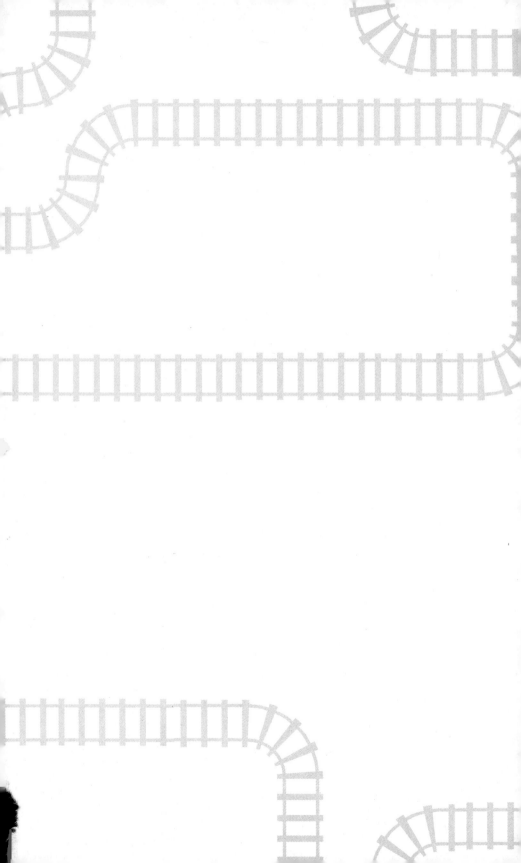